Season of the Great Bird

A Story of Hope and Redemption

mad+mama+publishing

Detroit

A Story by Maryann Lawrence

With Watercolor Paintings by Andrew Lawrence

ISBN 978-0-359-94442-2

Chapter I

In the Days of Peace, when all Living Things lived in harmony, the youthful Earth knew but one season – the Season of Beauty.

But the Living Things did not call the seasons by name then, as every beautiful day was as the next and no one bothered to count them.

In the Days of Peace, flowers always bloomed, trees grew thick with green leaves, the waters were warm, and the Living Things lacked for nothing.

On the ground, animals of every sort roamed the Earth, and the streams, rivers, lakes and oceans brimmed with life. Atop the trees many birds flew and sang their happy melodies. But it was the Bird of Many Colors whose song was sweetest of all.

The Bird of Many Colors was the oldest of any Living Thing. No creature, no plant or flower or tree, could recall a time when the Bird of Many Colors did not exist.

There was nothing the Bird did not know, there was nothing the Bird could not do, nothing the Bird did not see, nothing the Bird did not love.

It was the most beautiful, gentle and happy of all Living Things. For this it was called, also, the Bird of Love.

In those days the Earth was divided into many parts, and each part had its distinct population of particular trees, flowers, insects, animals and birds.

The Bird of Many Colors flew over every one of them at regular intervals, stopping for a time, guiding and instructing in matters of love and wisdom, and each Living Thing, no matter where it lived, eagerly awaited the Bird's arrival.

Chapter II

It came to pass that the Bird of Many Colors had not flown over a particular area for some time. At first it was only the youngest of Living Things that asked, "When will the Bird of Love come?" The question was repeated day and night until soon the elders were asking one another, "When will the Bird of Love come?"

When their question was not answered, the Living Things asked a new question: "Why doesn't the Bird of Love come to us?"

When this question could not be answered, the Living Things then asked, "What have we done to make the Bird of Love angry with us?" For they believed only a great offense could keep the beautiful bird away for so long.

Days and nights passed and still the Bird of Many Colors did not come. Before very long, one of the Living Things, a Butterfly named Pathena, turned to a tall Oak tree and asked, "What did you do to make the Bird of Many Colors stay away for so long?"

The Oak tree, which was very sad because the Bird of Love had still not come, answered, "It may well have been something you said."

At this Pathena became enraged and began gnawing at the Oak's leaves, making jagged holes in their smooth surface. The Oak tree shook its branches to get the Butterfly off its leaves, but Pathena merely flew away, though many other insects fell to the ground. Pathena returned with her family and, joined by the fallen insects, all rose up in vengeance against the tree.

Together they ravaged the helpless Oak until its leaves were full of holes and its branches shook with the weight of a multitude of angry insects.

Other trees threw nuts and berries to help the Oak, but this only enraged the insects more, and soon all the trees were under attack and many more creatures joined the fight.

Chapter III

Thus began the Terrible War and every Living Thing became engaged in battle. Insects ate the beautiful green leaves of the trees, birds and frogs and other small creatures devoured the insects. Animals fought one another.

The trees, shrinking from their attackers, bent low to the ground and the wind blew hard through their leaves. They used their fruits as weapons against the creatures – acorns, berries, fruit, chestnuts, cones, whatever could be projected – and so were not without blame.

Even the Creatures of the Sea fought against one another, causing the water to rise up in great torrential waves that crashed upon the shore and swallowed the smaller things that made their homes there.

The Terrible War continued without rest, without an end in sight, and malice enveloped the hearts of the once beautiful Living Things.

At that time there lived a Tall Pine, whose branches reached closest to the clouds, which was greatly respected by all the Living Creatures. Its needles were long and dark, and its lower branches always stretched out to shade a tired traveler from the hot sun.

For many years its upper trunk had been home to a family of Doves, and the Doves and the Tall Pine remained the only Living Things that did not engage in the atrocities carried out during the Terrible War.

Nonetheless, the Tall Pine suffered much. Its once lush needles fell to the ground. Poisonous vines tangled their slender stems around its trunk and strangled its weakened branches. Bugs of every kind infected what was left.

The War had gone on for many days and nights when finally the Tall Pine could stand no longer, and a great wail was heard as the tremendous tree crashed to its death. Its crash was as an earthquake and the Doves flew high into the sky. All Living Things stopped their fighting and mourned the death of that beloved tree.

It was a Dove that first saw the Bird of Many Colors as it fled the fallen Pine. How long had he been there, watching them? Nobody knew. In the silence, the Bird did not sing its beautiful song but instead gave forth a terrible cry, which touched the hearts of all Living Things.

Chapter IV

Then the Bird's colorful feathers turned to red and his wings fluttered angrily. The Red Bird flew above the Oaks, above the Birches, above the Maples and the Pines, and when he reached the highest point, he caused a strong, cold wind to blow over.

The Sky grew thick with black clouds until the Sun became invisible and all was dark. Rain pelted down from the clouds and stung the Living Creatures and some of the smallest were washed into the seas.

The Great Bird's fury was alive in the strong winds. It blew savagely and, for the first time in life, leaves of every tree became disengaged from their lofty homes. As they fell their cries were as dirges, solemn and repentant.

When finally, the rain relented, the Sky turned the drops to snow, and the leaves, shivering and wailing still, were buried beneath a blanket of bitter cold.

The Flowers, too, were helpless against the wind and cold. Frost covered their petals until soon they succumbed to the weight of the heavy snow. The waters froze over and the Creatures of the Sea were trapped below. The Creatures of the Land were left to find shelter for themselves in that frozen darkness and, in the days that followed, many Living Things died

Chapter V

The family of Doves which had lived in the Tall Pine had all perished but one. It was this Creature, the youngest Dove, which implored the Bird of Many Colors to release the Earth from its punishment, and the Great Bird's heart was deeply moved by the compassion of that small Creature.

"I cannot undo the damage the Living Things have already done. But I will grant you the Four Seasons of Life. This very day I shall leave you as you are and I will fly above the clouds forever, but when you see a Rainbow – a band of every color alighted in the Sky – you will know that the Day of Renewal is near.

"This Rainbow will mark the season of Spring, and new buds will grow and new creatures shall be borne to populate the Earth. The Bees will hum again, and the Swallows shall sing. When Doves pass over the Rainbow, you will remember that it was the smallest of these creatures that purchased for you the mercy I bestow and, for this, you shall call them Birds of Peace.

"The Butterflies, too, will brighten the Earth again with their colorful wings. But because of the cruelty of Pathena, he and his kin will be stripped of their colors. They shall be called Moths and will fly only in the darkest hours as a reminder to all Living Things that no light can shine in a heart of blackness.

"In the Season of Summer life will bloom to its full and the Earth shall become warm once more, as it was during the Days of Peace. This shall remind you that my love for you continues, and that I have not forgotten the happy days of our youth.

"The Season of Autumn shall follow Summer, and the winds will blow cooler. The leaves of the trees will change to yellow, crimson and orange. This will remind you of the beauty of my feathers, which shall no longer fly above you.

"The changing leaves will grow dry with the coming of the cold once more and fall to the ground as they did during the darkest days. Only the family of the heroic Tall Pine, whose death brought an end to the Terrible War, will be excluded and its seeds will spawn new breeds and their names shall be called Evergreen.

"Then begins the Season of Winter. Snow will fall to the ground and the waters will freeze, such as they have now. This is a reminder of the Terrible War. For it is only in remembering our failings that we can overcome them and be born anew."

With these words, the Bird of Many Colors left the Earth and flew up into the clouds and was never seen again. The waters began to thaw and the snow melted, and for many days a soft rain fell. Soon the Living Things saw in the Sky a ribbon of colors that spanned the tallest trees of the North to the smallest sprigs of the South, and the Living Things were happy once more.

Spring had come to them as the Bird of Love had promised. Though its Youth had passed, the Earth began life anew, as it would each Spring when the first shower of rain washes away all cold and darkness and brings with it a Rainbow of promise for all Living Things to come.

Maryann Lawrence lives in Southeast Michigan.

She writes poetry, essays and children's stories.

Illustrations were created by her son, Andrew Lawrence,

who lives in Washington D.C.